Frosty's New Friends

Frosty's New Friends

Based on the character and original song lyrics
by Steve Nelson and Jack Rollins

Illustrated by Richard Cowdrey

SCHOLASTIC INC.
New York Toronto London Auckland Sydney
Mexico City New Delhi Hong Kong Buenos Aires

ISBN 0-439-81646-7

12 11 10 9 8 7 6 5 4 3 2 1   5 6 7 8 9 10/0

Printed in the U.S.A.   08

This edition first printing, September 2005

Frosty the Snowman had to hurry on his way
but he waved good-bye, saying,
Don't you cry, I'll be back again some day.

Daddy closed the book.
"Did he? Did Frosty ever come back?"

"He certainly did,"
Daddy answered.
"I know because I was
there. I saw him."

It was late at night and I was in bed.
My little sister was fast asleep.
Suddenly, what did I hear?
A tap tap tapping at the window.

And who do you think was there? Why, Frosty himself.
"I'm back!" he cried.
In a flash, we got dressed and ran outside.

"I think they'd like to come and play too.
Don't you?" Frosty asked us.

Then, with a tip of his magic hat,
one, two, three . . .
the snowboy and the snowpup
were alive as you and me.

From the shed, we got our sled.

Wheeeeee!

We played Hide-and-Snow-Seek.
Frosty was It.
"One snowflake, two snowflakes,
three snowflakes . . ." he counted.

"Ready or not, here I come!"

"You want a snowball fight? Watch this!"
He tipped his hat again.

And when I threw the snowball, guess what?
It bounced!

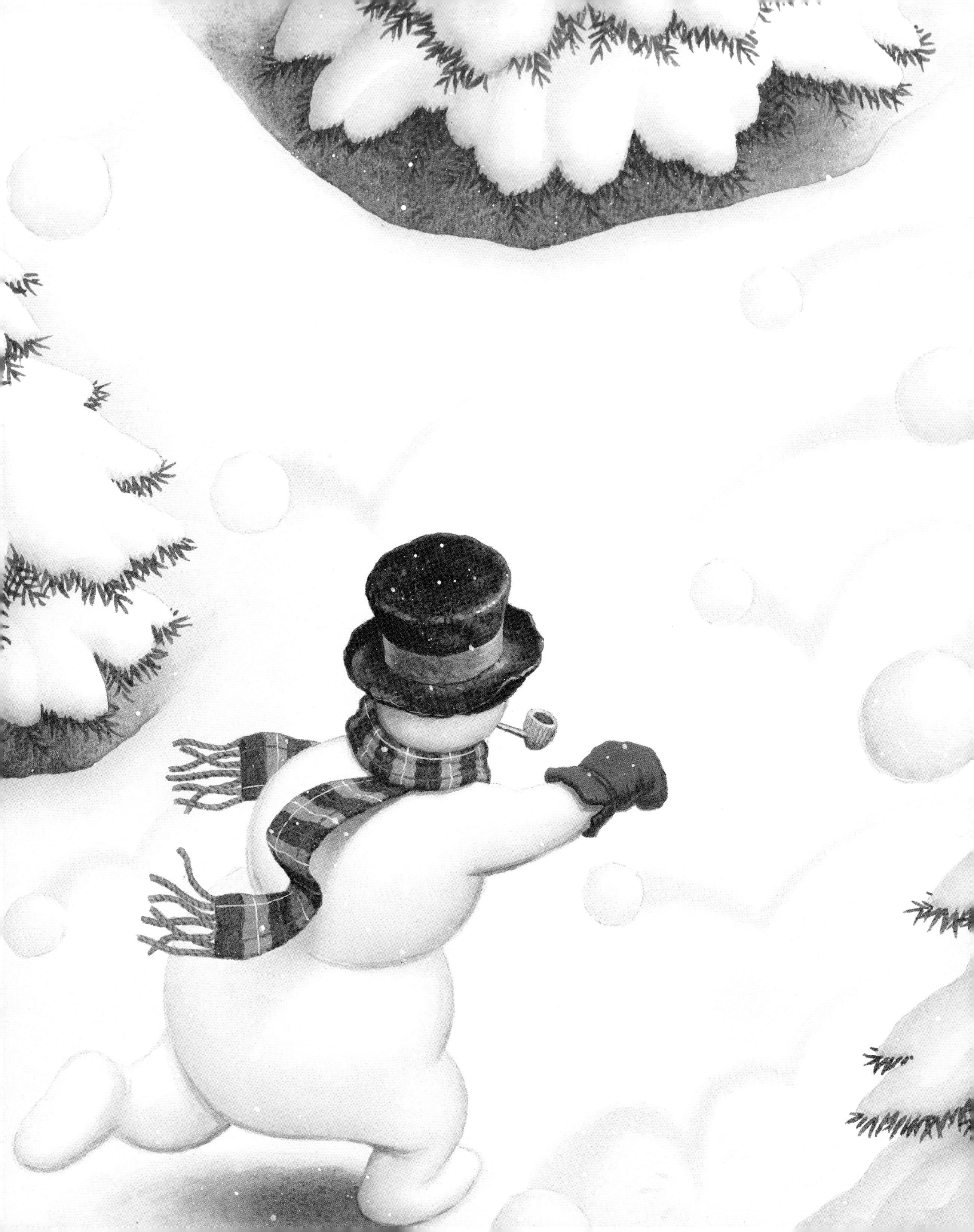

Snowballs were flying everywhere.

But where had the snowpup gone?
We looked all over.

And finally,
we found him . . .

. . . fast asleep.

"Oh, my! Time to say good-bye!" Frosty told us.
And away they went,

thumpety thump thump,
thumpety thump thump,
over the hills of snow.

"Will Frosty ever come back again?"
Daddy answered, "I wouldn't be at all surprised."